D1509288

Other Kipper books

Kipper
Kipper's Toybox
Kipper's Birthday
Kipper's Snowy Day
Where, Oh Where, is Kipper's Bear?
Kipper's Book of Colours
Kipper's Book of Opposites
Kipper's Book of Counting
Kipper's Book of Weather

First published 1999
by Hodder Children's Books,
a division of Hodder Headline plc,
338 Euston Road, London NW1 3BH

This hardback edition published 2000

10 9 8

ISBN 0 340 799250

A catalogue record for this book
is available from the British Library.
The right of Mick Inkpen to be identitfied
as the author of this work
has been asserted by him.

Printed in Hong Kong

Honk!

Mick Inkpen

Hodder
Children's
Books

A division of Hodder Headline

'Honk!' said the gosling.

'Where did you come from?' said Kipper.

'Honk!' said the gosling again.

'You can go in the bath!' said Kipper. 'Honk!' said the gosling to the plastic duck, which didn't reply.

'Do you like
     bubble bath?'
said Kipper.
     'Honk!' said the gosling,
blowing a bubble
     by accident.

'Can you only say
Honk!' said Kipper.
The gosling nodded.
And honked again.

I t honked
at the towel.
It honked
at the sponge.
It honked
at the hairdryer. . .

E specially when
it blew him
out of the bathroom!

And it honked
as it bumped
into Big Owl!
    'Are you all right?'
said Kipper.

But the gosling
didn't reply.
It didn't say 'honk'.
 It fell fast asleep,
without saying
 anything at all!